The Warrior Prince

Book 2 in the *Stay in the Castle* Series

By Pastor Jerry Ross

To order additional copies:
www.stayinthecastle.com
or call (812) 665-4375

All Scripture from the King James Bible
©2019 by Jerry Ross
All rights reserved

Printed in the United States of America

Introduction

Twenty years ago, I wrote the booklet, *Stay in the Castle*. From the onset, I never saw it as a gender-specific story. What I mean by that — to me, it has never been a "girlie book." I believe that young men can gain as much from it as young ladies. After all, if there is no prince on his way to the castle, then there is no motivation to "stay in the castle."

So, when someone would ask, "When are you going to write a guy's version of *Stay in the Castle?*" I would bristle a bit, then launch into my defense of the story's duel-gender benefits.

*"If there is no white-horsed rider, 'sitting straight and tall,' no knighted prince whose 'stance spoke of honor and character,' no young masculine royal eyes 'finding her in the shadows,' then there is no closing scene — there is no story. See, the story has both a princess **and** a prince."* End of discussion.

Most nodded politely but seemed totally unconvinced by my arguments.

So, for twenty years people have inquired by email, text, letter, and phone message — others, face to face — all asking for the prince's side of the story.

OK. I surrender. Here it is….

Pastor Jerry Ross

1 John 2:14-17

...I have written unto you, young men, because ye are strong, and the word of God abideth in you, and ye have overcome the wicked one. Love not the world, neither the things that are in the world. If any man love the world, the love of the Father is not in him. For all that is in the world, the lust of the flesh, and the lust of the eyes, and the pride of life, is not of the Father, but is of the world. And the world passeth away, and the lust thereof: but he that doeth the will of God abideth for ever.

Leaving the Castle

My father's embrace was strong, as if he would not let me go — perhaps he had changed his mind, or lost confidence in me. Then he spoke into my ear.

"Remember."

He held me at arm's length, stared hard into my eyes, then a softness touched his countenance — briefly, yes, but still it was there. Abruptly, he turned away followed by his royal guard — men who had whipped me, scolded me, trained me, challenged me, fought me, hardened me, and eventually, accepted me. None looked back. I stood alone now, at the castle's gate, myself, my stallion, my weapon, and my few provisions tied in a cloth bundle. As I turned to go, she came from the shadows.

"Mother."

"My son." She slipped her arm in mine and pulled me close. I suddenly thought how tiny she seemed. A few gray strands graced her crown as tiny wrinkles framed her eyes. But no age, no weakness touched her words.

"I knew this day would come, but I cannot say I am ready for it. I will pray for you, always. Ride tall, keep to the King's Highway, and remember who you are."

I stared after the castle lord, my father. "I do not know if I am ready. I'll never be the man he is, but I will try to honor his name."

"He does not need you to be who he is. He needs you to be the man God made you to be. He is proud of you."

My mind sped back over the last eight years. The day I turned twelve, it began — the hours of intense study, the days of physical training, the weeks out in the field, the mock battles, the victories, the failures — eight years' worth to prepare for today.

"He didn't say good-bye."

She smiled, ever wise, ever good. "Yes, he did. He just did it his way. Besides, good-byes are unnecessary. Now, walk with your mother."

The day was half spent, and I was anxious to leave, but I could not refuse her. My father was iron and steel — my mother, a soft blossom breeze and gentle bird's song. Of all that my father had accomplished, the best was taking this bride.

"Three things I ask — just three."

"Anything," I said and meant.

Her eyes probed mine, till she found my soul. "The dragon — you cannot let down your guard or underestimate his cunning. He will determine to stop you. All your father has taught you, you will need in that moment. Trust your sword, show no fear, resist... and *win*."

All I could manage was a nod.

"Your brother." Her eyes glistened. "I feel he is out there. A mother knows. Find him, if you can. Help him. Tell him we wait for him."

Three years ago, I had stood in the shadows and watched my mother hold strong to my older brother, standing where we now stood. I remember the intensity of her eyes as she said her goodbye, and now I wondered if the words she spoke to him then were some of the same she spoke now. We had not heard from him since, other than rumors — always the rumors.

"If I can, I will find him."

I thought she might not be able to continue, but under the rose petal exterior was an oak beam resolve. She turned and led me back to my waiting horse.

"You said there were three things."

She drew my head down to hers and kissed my cheek.

"Somewhere out there she waits."

I felt the heat of a blush, despising my reaction as it happened. It seemed so unmanly to know so little about such things. My strict father and ever-alert mother had kept tight reins on me. No girlfriends, no village parties, no flirting, no…. anything. The castle's stable boys knew more about the secrets of women than I, and sometimes laughed at my ignorance and innocence. It had been, at times, a point of contention between my parents and me, but there was no give on their part. So, I had set it aside, and prepared.

"Who?" I asked in unbelief.

"The One." She smiled as her finger traced the scar on my cheek — one rightly earned during sword practice when I was barely fifteen. Just a moment of distraction and loss of focus had left me bleeding and embarrassed. My mother had tended it that evening, telling me it would make me more handsome — and hopefully wiser.

"I know your father and I have kept your attention… elsewhere. We did so on purpose. The battle to which you ride has produced heroes and corpses. The enemy is more formidable than you can imagine. We insisted that your young-man years be focused on preparation, patience and practice. There are victories for you to win for the King. You will understand shortly why we reared you as we did. You will understand and be glad."

Her voice then softened. "But now, you are of age. As you travel to your destiny, along the way, somewhere, she waits. She too has been preparing — preparing her soul for yours. She will help make you stronger, braver, and better. Because of her, you will gain favor."

She placed her hand over my heart. "As you go, you listen to that guiding voice, and you find her. Then someday, you bring her back so I can meet her, and hold my grandchildren."

I did not know what to say, so I wrapped my strong arms

around her slight frame and held her. She cried; I did not. As much as I would miss her, I wanted to see where the King's Highway would take me, and now, I was even more eager to ride.

The King's Highway

The world was vaster than I had imagined. The Highway led through dark valleys and lush highlands. It wound narrowly upward through mountainous stretches, then slashed downward, right and left through rocky terrain. Of a night, I'd sleep beneath the stars, my sword close by, but my mind far away. I'd ponder the words of the *Book of Lessons* I'd hidden in my heart as a boy. Back then, I had not always enjoyed repeating them over and over, but now they came back strong, especially at night — maybe because I was alone and now listened for them.

The way was not always clear. Twice the Highway seemed to split, going in two different directions. I sat my steed and quieted my heart, remembering my mother's advice. Sometimes it took a while, but that guiding voice always led.

I was a trained warrior, yet still untested in battle. Only once, in the first few weeks, did I need to unsheathe my sword. I came upon three vagabonds harassing a young man and his sisters. The lad was standing up to them bravely, but the odds were too great, and as I rounded the bend, two pinned him to the ground as their companion grabbed the oldest of the girls. The two restraining the boy saw me, turned coward and ran into the forest as I approached. The other saw me too late, so I knocked him to the ground, then sheathed my sword, and proceeded to give him a well-deserved thrashing. When I was done, he limped away bloody and chastened. Bandits haunted the road, worthless men who preyed on those who were weaker or fewer than they, and I determined to use my strength and skills against them. The boy — bruised eye, bloodied lip, but smiling — thanked me. I shook his hand and honored him for defending his sisters, then I mounted and rode on.

Besides these rare evils, the way was tranquil, and it was easy to forget the challenges that awaited me. No war ravaged here, no enemy seemed to threaten. The few travelers I met carried no tales of the dragon or his destruction. Still, every morning I practiced my sword skills, hearing in my mind the voice of my father, urging and encouraging, correcting and challenging. Home was weeks behind me, but his words still instructed me.

Occasionally, I would come to a castle and stop for the night. I had been taught to seek lodging with those of royal descent and all seemed to know of my father and held him in high regard. These lords helped direct me, encourage me, provision me, and advise me on my journey. I never lingered, for duty called me forward, and again — for a time — the road was my home.

Something else urged me on — the thought of... her. She was out there, somewhere, of this I was absolutely sure.

The Village

It had been three full moons since I had left home. The sun had not shown for several days, and the air was charged with unrest. I crested a steep hill and two sights accosted me, one from above and the other below. Dark clouds churned the skies, riding the wind toward me, and below, a village churned in similar chaos. This was the largest village I had come to since I had left home. The King's Highway looped around it, but a dirt road, wide and well used, broke away and led down to it. My provisions were depleted, and weather threatened, so I made a quick decision and turned toward the village. My horse fought me, as I guided it toward the buildings huddled below. A still, small voice within seemed to give warning, yet I was without provisions and needing shelter, and so proceeded downward.

As I neared the village, people were scurrying in all directions, gathering in whatever the storm might destroy. Shutters were pulled tight, and doors bolted as mothers called for their children. A man yelled something at me that the wind snatched away, as he waved and pointed me toward his barn. I rode my horse through its low door, dismounted, then latched the door and raced toward the house. The stranger stood at the door, urging me, as rain and hail hurled downward. The door was bolted behind me, and slowly, my eyes began to adjust to the light of a single smoky lantern.

Eyes glowed from the darkness, as an equal number of dogs and people stared in curiosity. An eerie silence hung with the smoke, broken only by the storm outside and the low growls of the large beasts within.

"You aren't from around here, are you, lord?" a man's voice said from the darkness.

The man who had let me in, stepped up beside me, laying his hand on my shoulder. "No, he's not. He rode down from the King's Highway, and a good thing too. Now make room for our guest... give up a chair!" he shouted at an old woman to my left. She cowered, then bolted into the darkness, as the man pushed me toward the stool.

"Sorry about that. We don't get many visitors — my family half forgot their manners." He began to pull at my cloak. "Let me take this and your sword..."

I pulled sharply away, stepping back to face the man fully, my hand on the sword's hilt. "I thank you for inviting me in from the storm, but all that I have I will keep, and no man takes my sword."

Dark anger flashed in his eyes, but his practiced smile never wavered. "Of course, lord, never meant any harm. Just want you to be comfortable."

My warrior senses switched on full ready. Deep-throated growls increased as several large beasts stood, agitated by my quick actions. Three young men also stood to their feet. No one breathed as I held the man's gaze, my mind quickly calculating my chances if violence was needed.

Then a curtain parted in the far corner, and out of the darkness, out of the smoke and the clutter, walked an angel. Her presence commanded the room, while her smile dispelled the tension. She stopped just a foot from me, her eyes capturing mine, curious and searching. She reached out and traced my scar with her finger, then her hand dropped to rest on my sword arm.

"Please, you must be famished. Come, sit with me." She was the most beautiful girl I had ever seen.

****

Thunder jolted the queen awake from her troubled sleep, and she instinctively reached over to where her husband lay. He was not there. A lightning flash outlined his silhouette, as he stood staring out of their bedroom window. She moved beside him and took his arm.

He drew her close. "The dragon preys on such nights."

"You trained the boy well. He knows what is right, and the guiding voice travels with him. We must pray and trust."

"We believed the same of his brother, and now, three years have passed. And still no word, only whispers." He stared into the raging storm, as if he might see as only God can. "Where are my sons tonight?"

Two bodies sharing one heart knelt together on the flagstone floor. In tender embrace, a mother's heart cried, and a lord's voice rose, both imploring the throne of grace.

****

Long after the warrior prince had returned to the barn to care for his steed and prepare his bed in the loft, the girl once again commanded the house. This time, there was no smile.

"Why is it always violence with you? He would have killed half of you before you could have overwhelmed him!"

Her older brother stammered, "Did you see his horse? We could get five years' wages for the animal. We should have taken him!"

A young cousin barked through rotten teeth, "The dogs! We could have loosed the dogs on him. A man like that has to be carrying gold coins. And that sword is worth a fortune. I say we wait till he's asleep and rush the barn!"

The young woman shook her head at their foolishness. She was beautiful, and she knew it. It had always been her power. Her voice lectured them like children, "He's a prince and a warrior. He's spent his whole life training to deal with the likes of you." She then ran her hands down her sides, smoothing out the patched dress that clung to her.

"He's also a man. You leave him to me. We'll have all he owns, and he'll be glad to give it."

****

I awoke an hour before sunrise. The rain no longer pattering the roof, instead the world had grown quiet after the storm — as if waiting for something.

"Parisa." I pronounced her name slowly, out loud. Time had stopped when she walked into the room last night. Instantly, the situation went from perilous to peaceful — even the canines went calm. Later, the two of us had huddled together on a bench outside on the porch, the rain by then having slowed to a steady soaking. She engaged me in conversation, and soon I found myself opening up to her. The bench was small, so a few times our knees touched, but she never seemed to notice. I'd never met anyone like her — irreverent, wickedly funny and perfectly comfortable in her own skin. And so beautiful.

I tried to picture her back home in my parents' castle, sharing a meal with my family. In that setting she seemed so out of place. Would my parents approve? Would they like her? Surely, if they got to know her, they would see how special she was. The day I left, my mother had said, "Find her. She is waiting." Well, maybe Parisa was the one.

I heard the barn door squeak open, and her gay laughter broke the silence.

"Wake up, sleepy head! The sun's coming up over the mountains. Can't miss that, come walk with me." I vaulted down from the loft, landing softly in front of her. Her hair was still wet, freshly washed, smelling of lilac. I started strapping on my sword when she reached out and playfully grabbed my wrist.

"You don't need that. The people here are rough, but kind and good. You are safe here."

Twenty years raised in my father's palace — the last eight in warrior training — answered her without hesitation. "I never go anywhere without my sword. Never."

She hesitated just for a moment, her eyes narrowing slightly, then she threw back her head and laughed. "Very well. As you wish." She grabbed my hand and pulled me into the predawn morning. I was taken back by her boldness, but it seemed natural to her, so I let her lead. We walked uphill toward the high meadow. "Why would it hurt to leave your sword? There is no danger here."

"The dragon and the destruction he brings — you never know where or when he will appear."

"You believe in this dragon?"

"Well, of course. Don't you?"

"I've never seen one." She walked awhile, a knowing smile playing at her lips. "The old women of the village tell of a hairy beast that lives in the hills to the east. As a child, I used to have nightmares of it. Then I grew up and discovered they use these tales to keep the children from wandering too far away.

Old woman tales to scare children into obeying."

"Are you saying my parents would lie to me?"

She stopped and looked at me, suddenly serious, "Oh, no. I am sure they would not view it as such. But sometimes adults tell us things to — you know — control our behavior. I mean, are you absolutely sure the dragon exists? Have you seen him?"

I walked on beside her, glad she was there, but disturbed by her words. No, I thought, I have never seen the dragon. But why all the years of preparation, of instruction, of warning?

"Where were you headed to when the storm came?"

"I'm off to join the King's army. To fight the war against the…. enemy."

"Is that what you want to do?"

"It is my duty."

"But didn't anyone ever ask you what *you* wanted to do? Don't you get a say in your life?"

By now, we had reached the summit and she turned me around toward the east. The sun was torching the morning clouds on the horizon — red blazed and orange burned above the yellow embers' glow. "I think you are strong and brave and kind. And I think you should live whatever life you choose. What *you* choose. Not someone else. Do what makes you happy."

She stood close to me, and we watched the sunrise for several moments, then she sighed deeply. "I'm hungry! You know what I do when I'm hungry?"

I shook my head.

"I eat!!" Again, she threw her head back and laughed out loud. "Come on, I'll show you a short cut to the village." And with that, she raced ahead, barefoot and beautiful, down the hill. I smiled, then chased her, completely taken with this happy, glorious girl.

****

Forest fragments and building debris littered the village streets. Axes rang as downed trees were turned into firewood. Everywhere, people were picking up their scattered belongings, patching roofs and righting overturned carts. A woman shrieked, then wailed, as her lost daughter was found lifeless at the forest edge, struck down by a large limb. A ragged mule hobbled up the road on three legs, the fourth dangling. A man was being carried from the tavern to his home, a bloody bandage wrapped around his head. He moaned, more drunk than hurt, and cursed aloud.

I stopped. His voice seemed familiar.

Parisa pulled at my arm. "Come on, I'm famished."

I pulled away and ran to the men who bore the drunkard. I grabbed at him and lowered him to the ground, as the men protested around me.

"Angus?"

He looked back through glazed eyes, not comprehending, unable to answer. I patted his face and repeated his name.

Parisa now was leaning over my shoulder. "Who is he?" I glanced up at her, then back to him as tears blurred my vision.

"He... is my brother."

****

That evening found me sitting beside his bed, praying for him to recover his wits. I had helped carry him to his home, a low-roofed, former pig shed that now contained a bed, a table and chair, and little else. His few "friends" told me his story when they stopped by to check on him.

Three years ago, as I did, he too had ridden into this village. Some men had befriended him, talked him into staying and investing in a business deal. Days later, they beat and robbed him and left him for dead. His left leg had been broken and had never properly healed. Penniless and injured, the tavern owner took pity and gave him this shed in return for sweeping the floors and tending bar. That is when the drinking started. Seems there had also been a woman or two, but they soon tired of a drunk. I could not believe what he had become, and I fought back the tears as I considered what this would do to my parents.

His eyes opened, fought to focus, then rested on me. He sat up slowly, then reached out for me. I embraced him, and he wept. He then gathered himself and shoved me away.

"What are you doing here?" he spat at me.

"I was on my way to join the King's army and I..."

"You what? Left the King's Highway? Stopped here? Are you mad?"

"There was a storm..."

"So, ride through it! What were you taught? Never leave the King's Way. Never!" His eyes blazed, and I thought for a moment he might strike me. He then bowed his head, ashamed. "You need to leave."

"But I..."

"You need to leave now!"

I stood, no longer his lesser brother, but now in the full strength of my youth. "No. I will leave when I choose, and not before. And not without my brother!"

Parisa came in and stood beside me, both of us looking down at the shell of a once mighty warrior. He began to quiver as drunkards will, riding the pain as he curled up into a ball. He screamed in agony, then at God, and then he cursed me again and again for being there. I listened till I could not stand to hear him, then shouted over him, "I'll be back, when you sober up and get a civil tongue in your head." I turned and walked out, angry — so angry at him. How could he do this? How could he be this?

Parisa caught up with me as I stormed down the village street. Nothing made sense, and I felt the fool. What was real anymore? Duty? Honor? The Warrior's Way? Was it all a tall tale, a fanciful dream? Dragons and battle and victory — or was this village and others like it all there was?

"What are you going to do?" she cooed.

"I have to leave. I need to get out of here."

She grabbed hold of my arm, slowing my steps. "But you can't. Not yet. Give it some time. Your brother, he needs you. You have to stay." She jerked me to a halt, then leaned into my chest. "I need you."

I stood in the street, as the villagers stared from their hovels and shops. My mind whirled in circles. I had no idea what to do. No idea.

Parisa's closeness suddenly felt wrong. I had been taught better than this. I pushed her gently away. "I need time to think." And with that, I walked alone up the slope to where we had watched the day's birth, sat down and wept till I was empty. I lay back, my mind a blank, till the sun warmed me to sleep.

****

She crashed through the door in a rage. Her brother and cousins jumped to their feet. "He says he's leaving! The fool found his brother, and now he's determined to play the hero!"

"Has he gone?"

"No, he's up in the meadow. Pushed me away! Said he needed to think." She paced back and forth like a panther. "Pushed me away. No man has ever done that!" She paused, then decided. "Get your weapons. Give me a few minutes to go speak to him. Slip up quietly — quietly, you fools! When you hear me call out, you come in and kill him. He's not leaving. His horse and his gold will give us a new start. Now, get ready!"

Eight men in all raced for their weapons then watched from the window as she climbed the slope. They marked her path in their minds, then huddled together to plan their attack.

****

Angus faded in and out, unable to focus. Was it a dream, or a drunken hallucination? Had it been real? He fought as he had not fought in years, clawing his way to full consciousness. He struggled to stand. It wasn't a dream, his brother was here! And if so, he was in danger.

He fell hard as he started for the door. Tears mingled with cold sweat, as a wave of nausea took him — the room spinning as he heaved up nothing. His forehead rested on the dirt floor, his body convulsed until the tremor passed. He fought to control his breathing and quiet his mind and emotions. Then he did something he had not done in three years.

He prayed.

****

I woke as she knelt beside me, her hand resting on my shoulder. The aroma of the meadow grass mingled with her floral scent made it hard to think. I wanted to quit, just give up and lie here forever. At home, my days were planned for me, my decisions simple, my values strong, my counselors many. Life was so easy. Right so plain. Wrong so… wrong! Back home...

I softly prayed, "God, help me. I don't know what to do."

In answer, I saw my father's face. "Remember."

My mother's face appeared beside his, her words following his one. "The dragon — you cannot let down your guard or underestimate his cunning. He will determine to stop you. All your father has taught you, you will need in that moment. Trust your sword, show no fear, resist… and *win*."

I sat up suddenly, everything clear. I knew what to do because for the first time in days, I remembered who I was.

"What's wrong?"

"Parisa, I'm sorry." I looked into her eyes, feeling nothing but guilt. I had misled this poor, innocent girl. "I have to go."

"Go where? What are you going to do?"

"This is not who I am, I've been a fool. I am sorry — this is not my life, not my destiny." As I tried to stand, she pushed me off balance and threw herself on me, clawing at my face.

"You think you can just leave me, just throw me away like a piece of garbage!" I was so shocked, that at first, I did not even defend myself. Her hands then grabbed at my sword, as she tried to wrestle it out of its sheath.

'Kill him! Kill him, now!" She was shrieking like a vulture and fighting like a lioness, as around me, men charged, weapons drawn.

I had at times complained about the hours of sword training and battle drills, but I thanked God for them now. My warrior's training took hold as I leapt to my feet, sweeping Parisa away from me with my strong left arm, flinging her several yards into meadow. My right hand unleashed my sword. I parried the first attacker's sword thrust, then rammed my fisted hilt into his face, splattering blood and breaking teeth, putting him down for good. The second man came in fast, swinging his sword at my body, cutting my left side as I twisted away. My back stroke grazed his shoulder, wounding him slightly.

Parisa was cursing me and urging them to kill me, and as I looked into her eyes I saw murder.

One man was down, another wounded but coming, the other six more cautious. I had superior training, but they were many and determined. I felt the blood seeping down my left side but could not stop to check the seriousness of my wound.

They taunted as they circled around me. I prayed for strength to defeat them, and if not, a brave death. And then on some unseen signal, they attacked.

As they did, I heard a warrior's cry, one both familiar and savage. From my left came my brother into the fray, screaming and slashing into our enemies. Two went down quickly, then he was inside what was left of the circle. Our backs touched, and we faced our opponents as we had been trained under our father's watchful eye. How many times had we prepared for this moment? How many times had our father's royal guard outnumbered us, circled us, taunted us, and trained us to watch each other's back and win against superior numbers?

I glanced over my shoulder at my brother's rusty, borrowed weapon.

"Nice sword."

"It will do for the likes of these. I almost feel sorry for them."

Their courage was ebbing, but Parisa's screams drove them forward, so they came one last time. And our swords sang, as we danced the warrior's dance. The battle joy possessed us and soon three more were down, and those left were limping away. The danger passed, so I turned to Angus and embraced his emaciated frame. He weakened suddenly, and I held him up.

"Don't quit on me now. We need to get out of here."

We leaned on each other, dragging our swords as we walked off the hill. I looked back at the girl I thought I had loved and saw nothing but hatred in those once soft eyes. I had been a fool. As I turned away, the scar on my cheek began to throb.

****

Somehow, we made it to the barn, and saddled my stallion. No man tried to stop us as we rode double out of the village and back onto the King's Highway. Three years ago Angus entered this village — for me, two days, yet it seemed a lifetime.

I could feel his body in front of mine begin to shake. The

rum's poison was ravaging him again. Still, we must ride. Distance was our salvation, and I dare not stop. The horse was strong, as it had been cared for by men who thought it would soon be theirs. Time ceased to exist as the horse plodded on.

Hours later I woke, still mounted, the horse grazing along the side of the highway, my grip still strong upon my brother. He needed rest — we both did. I slid off, then led the horse into a willow thicket, where I found a small spring of clean, fresh water. As I lifted him off the horse, and lay him on my cloak, Angus mumbled something I could not understand. He was red hot, and delirium had set in. I poured water into his mouth, and he coughed some down, then fell into a tortured sleep.

I disrobed and checked my wound, an ugly gash that still seeped fresh blood. I washed it, then gathered the herbs I had been taught to use, mixed them with mud, and caked it over my wound. Tearing strips from my shirt, I wrapped my body, embracing the pain, then lay back exhausted. Finally, I fell asleep as our parents' prayers stood guard that night.

Rest and Recovery

Two days later, I rounded a bend and saw ahead a welcome sight — a castle, and the banners flying above its ramparts told me these were my father's allies. My horse trudged toward the gate, as I clung to my brother. His condition had worsened, and I feared for his life. My left side throbbed, and the horse stumbled, then regained its footing. The gates opened, and strong men ran to us, then caught us, as I fell from the saddle into blackness.

****

I awoke in strange surroundings, not knowing that I had slept for two days. It took another week in bed to recover from my wounds. I sat several evenings with the lord of the castle and told him all that had happened, including my poor decisions and lack of good judgment. I was ashamed, but needed to unburden myself. This good man listened without judgment or condemnation, then read to me passages out of the *Book of Lessons*. The words healed my heart and reestablished my thinking.

The lord showed no small kindness to my brother and me. He told me what he knew of the road ahead, warned of its perils, and reminded me to be vigilant. "The dragon destroys much of our land and decimates many of our people."

This puzzled me. I had not noticed in my travels any of the tell-tale signs of war's aftermath — no scorched fields, no burned out homes, no meadows marred with fresh graves — yet he insisted the dragon's destruction was everywhere.

"In time you will see it and know." This was all the explanation he would give.

The lord also spoke of other castles, other lords whom I should meet on my journey — good men who ruled well and lived by the *Book of Lessons*.

I asked him if he knew where the King's army was encamped. He extended his arm and swept it in all directions. Then smiled. "Perhaps the best thing for you to do is to go and see the King himself."

"Does he live near here?"

"Not far. Maybe ten days' journey."

"Is that where he trains his army?"

"His lords train men for the King, as your father trained you. The King then gives a place of service to those who prove themselves worthy. His time is spent on more important things."

I wondered what could be more important than leading warriors and defeating the enemy but checked my tongue. He could see my curiosity and explained further.

"The King spends most of his time traveling the kingdom,

gathering orphans and outcasts — he has even been known to purchase slaves from their cruel masters. He takes them home to his castle, gives them his name and rears them as his own."

I had never heard of such a thing and struggled to comprehend it. I enquired how my brother fared, and the kind lord encouraged me to check on him myself. I stood to go, but then stopped to ask one last question.

"My lord, I was told the King had a daughter, one of a pure heart and renowned virtue. Do you know if this is true?"

He smiled. "The King has many daughters, all adopted and all precious in His sight. But yes, there is one in particular whose kindness and virtue mirrors that of her Father. And if what I hear is true, she would be about your age."

I thanked him again, then left to check on my brother. He was far from well, but slowly recovering. Three years spent destroying the body temple is not fixed in a few weeks. The first ten days were a nightmare as his body fought free of rum's hold, and now he needed to rebuild his strength. I planned to stay till he could travel with me, but he would not hear of it.

"You must go, for you are needed by the King's army. I would only slow you."

"But I need you. I will wait until you are stronger, and we will ride together."

"Your path is not mine. You must go forward, I must go back." At first, I thought he meant to the village, and my anger rose, but he smiled and placed a hand on my arm. "No, little brother. Not back to that, not ever. I need to go back home. There are things that will never be right until I make them right with our father. When I am able, I will ride home. And then in God's time, I will come find you."

I knew he was right, but I still wished for his company. "So, again, I must ride alone."

"Ride, yes, but never alone. Your training, our father's instruction, our mother's wisdom, the lessons you have learned, and my prayers — all will ride with you. God's hand is strong upon you, little brother. Now go; there are battles to win and, if I am not mistaken, a young lady to find."

My embarrassment made him laugh, and he embraced me. "Godspeed. Ride tall, keep to the King's Highway..."

"... and remember who you are," I finished for him. I stood to leave. "Angus, back there — you saved my life."

Tears rimmed his eyes. "And you mine."

As I rode away, I looked back to see my brother limping along the castle's ramparts, watching me go. He would have to ride back past the village — past many villages — between here and home. The temptation could not be avoided, and I whispered a prayer that he would be strong. Then, I focused westward and followed the King's Highway.

The Road Ahead

The next several weeks, I made good progress. Several times I would pass within sight of a village, but always kept to the King's Highway. There were village travelers along the way, and for short distances we would traverse together and talk. Many knew nothing else but village life, so it was a joy to tell them about castles and kingdoms and good lords and better ways. Some thought I told fanciful tales, believing only what they could see around them.

Occasionally there were those who had heard of the King, but the best stories they told were of his noble daughter. Her reputation of kindness and gentleness reflected that of her father's and I increasingly longed to meet her.

Most of all, I loved talking to the children who would gather along the King's Highway, near whatever village they lived. I would share my food with them, or pass out a few copper coins, but more importantly, I shared with them some of the stories and lessons my parents had taught me. Most were poorly cared for, some even bore marks of abuse, and I pitied their hard existence. As I rode, I thought of the kind King who was rumored to take in orphans and free chained slaves.

The memories of Parisa sometimes rode with me for a few miles. At first, I was angry at her deceit, but the more I thought of her, my anger turned to sadness and pity. She was once one of these young girls along the Highway, yet life had taken a beautiful little girl and twisted her into a bitter, greedy and hateful young woman. I had come so close to falling in love with someone who, I now know, would have made my life miserable. I imagined how much different her life might have been if the King had found her as a little girl — found her and rescued her from what she now had become.

That night I found a small castle and enjoyed the company of a good lord. He knew the location of the King's castle and confirmed the stories of his extraordinary kindness.

"Just the other day, I was at the local market and was told the King had attended the slave auction there last month. Seven slaves had been sold, and he purchased them all, paying an extraordinary price for each. He then gave them their freedom. Two were children — a young boy and a young girl — who had no place to go, so he purchased each a pony, and they rode with him back to his castle. One man overheard him tell the children, 'You are now a prince and a princess.' Imagine! The idea of making slaves into royalty."

I asked of his daughter. Did she really exist, and were the stories of her goodness true?

He hesitated. "I do not want to bear a tale that may not be true. Yes, she exists. And yes, for years she was the talk of the kingdom and the picture of virtue. She may still be all that and more, but..."

"But what?"

"I will not repeat foolish rumors. People like to gossip, especially those jealous of royalty. I'm sure you will find her an extraordinary young lady." After that, he would say no more.

The next morning, we said our goodbyes. "Go straight ahead, you'll arrive at his castle by tomorrow morning." I left, anxious to meet the King and, if God willed, the princess.

The King's Castle

A hard day's travel and a short night's rest later, I was closing in on my destination. I left before the sun was up, hoping to arrive at the castle with the dawning of a new day.

I crested the hill just as the sun rose behind me and looked into the valley below. The morning rays painted the castle gold, and I knew I had found the King. My horse sensed my excitement, for it broke into a gallop as we neared. Behind the castle, there were children of all races and all ages preparing for the day. They performed their chores with youthful joy, and their laughter was musical. Never had I seen a happier place. I sat for a moment taking it all in, then dismounted and knocked on the castle door. Within minutes, the King himself stepped out. I bowed, then introduced myself.

"What brings you here, young man?"

For the last three days, I had practiced my words. "For eight years, I have trained in my father's house, to be a warrior prince. With his blessing, I left to join the King's army, to advance the cause of good and fight back the dragon and the evil he would spread. I know I still have much to learn, but I would offer my sword, my loyalty and my allegiance to you, your Highness." I then knelt, awaiting his answer.

"Stand, my son." I obeyed. "I know of your training, and of your father. The life you request is a difficult one. The dragon is destroying many in the kingdom, and it will take a young man who possesses great wisdom and greater courage to defend against him."

"I can only promise to do my best."

"Yes." The King looked into my soul. "Your best. That is what will be required. Young man, do you trust me?"

"With all of my heart."

"Then trust what I ask and obey. You still have much to learn. You look, but you do not always see. You listen, but you do not always hear. But I see that your heart is pure." He looked upon me with great affection. "Continue down the King's Highway. I want you to travel the kingdom until you find and face the dragon. When you have done so, return, and I will have a place for you in my army."

I had come so far, and this was not what I expected. "But how will I find the dragon? And how can I defeat him?"

"Listen to the guiding voice. Remember the words of the *Book of Lessons.* Lean heavily upon the wisdom your parents imparted to you. And have faith. Above all, your journey must be one of faith."

I knew I was being dismissed but risked a few more questions. "It is true, your Highness, that you rescue village orphans and adopt them as your children?"

He smiled, "It is."

"And that you buy up slaves and give them their freedom, and if needed, give them a home?"

He spread his arms out toward the children and teenagers surrounding the castle. "All of these you see were once as you described. They are no longer slaves, outcasts and orphans, but princes and princesses. They are my children — they bear my name and all that I have is available to them." He looked upon them with a love I could not comprehend.

"Your Highness, I do not want to sound presumptuous…"

"You may ask me whatever is in your heart."

"Many people have spoken of one of your daughters, an unusual and amazing young lady of great virtue. Does she exist? Is she here?"

A great sadness shadowed his countenance. My question produced in his eyes such grief that I instantly regretted asking. I felt a trespasser into his soul's most secret sorrow.

"Yes, she exists. And I love her as I always have. But, no, she is not here. You see, I gather these my children. I adopt them, love them, teach and train them to be noble, and virtuous, and good. I have a plan for their lives, and if they follow this plan, it always leads them to great purpose and greater happiness. But they must choose it. Each must choose between my will and what the world offers instead."

He paused for a long moment, lost in a painful memory. I thought he would not finish. "Yes, she was all you have heard — kind and noble and of great virtue. But she was deceived by the dragon and lured away into this world. I love her, will always love her — and she will always be my daughter — but, no my young friend, she is not here, and she is not what she once was."

His eyes wandered to a village in the distance. I followed his gaze to a shack on the river's edge, just across the bridge. In the shadow of the porch, I could just make out a feminine form.

****

She awoke with the dawn, not knowing that it was a year to the day since her departure. Her back hurt. "Just part of being in your last month of pregnancy," the village women had told her. Rising from her bed with difficulty, her husband muttered something in his half drunken state. He had come home only hours before and they had argued — again. Oh, well, after the baby is born maybe things will get better.

There was still a house to clean and chores to do. Picking up a straw broom, she walked outside to sweep the front porch. Their house was small and set at the edge of town, not far from the bridge where her then charming young man had waited that first night. Her eyes followed the path up to her Father's castle. The King had still found little ways to show her that he had not forgotten her; that she was still loved. But what he had said was true. Nothing was the same.

Her eyes wandered to the east, to spend a few minutes watching the sunrise — a simple pleasure that she shared alone each morning. Squinting against its brightness, she returned to the job at hand, first glancing absently up the castle road.

Her heart seemed to stop, gripped as if by a strong hand. The broom quivered in her grasp. Far down the road came a white horse, its rider sitting straight and tall. He seemed to be coming out of the sun. The horse quickened its pace as it neared the castle, sensing the excitement of its master. Her heart began to beat again, now loud and in rhythm to the pounding hoofs. He reined his mount to a stop outside the castle's front gate. She could not make out his features, but his stance spoke of honor and character. He knocked on the front door, *her* front door not that long ago. The King stepped out to greet him, and she watched as they conversed; watched as the King spoke with his hands, and then motioned toward the village. Involuntarily, she took a step back into the shadow of the porch.

The noble prince listened carefully, his strong shoulders sagging in disappointment and sadness. Shaking the King's hand and receiving from him a consoling hug, he mounted his horse. He looked toward her village home, his eyes finding her in the shadow. For a moment, their eyes locked. Then pointing his mount back toward the sun, he rode away into its brightness.

She felt the hot tears on her arms and hands long before it occurred to her that she was crying. *Nothing*, she thought, *will ever be the same.*

****

I rode east up to the King's Highway, then turned westward with a heavy heart — a sadness I could not shake for many days. I relived every moment, every word of my encounter with the King. Never had I seen such sorrow, such pain in any man as I saw when he spoke of his wayward daughter. I found myself hating the dragon, who seemed to exist only to hurt and destroy. If he could deceive a girl so pure, so full of promise and virtue, then I must be more vigilant than I had been to this point.

Everything about the King was good and right. That he had taken the time to talk to me and answer my questions was more than I could understand. I wanted to be like him yet knew that I fell so short. I rode away, excited to obey the King's orders, but unsure of all that he willed for my life.

I prayed for wisdom, for Angus, for Parisa, and then fervent prayers for the fallen princess. I finished, more determined to carry out my mission and perform my duty. So much destruction... the dragon must be found, and he must be destroyed.

The Dark Village

For the next year, I rode the King's Highway. I was keen to see, really see — and hear, really hear. Without a specific destination, I focused less on where I was going, and more on where I was. I lingered and listened to the people that I met along the way and tried to see them through the eyes of the King.

At times, I drew my sword against evil. But most of the time, the action required was not what I envisioned a warrior's life to be — a chance to help a widow by paying her rent, a few days spent helping a farmer get in his crops, or an opportunity to give children a ride to a local market. Always, in each case, I would tell them about the King. I wanted the people to know him as I knew him, to understand how blessed they were to have him, and to tell of his great acts of love and kindness.

Yet in all this, I never forgot my mission. I asked about the dragon wherever I rode. Not once did I find someone who had seen him, nor could I pin down the location of his lair. I was failing in my mission, and I felt a keen disappointment in myself.

Those who lived along the King's Highway possessed the strongest faith and lived the most blessed lives. Yet far off the road, down dark lanes and through choked forest paths were dark villages. In this part of the kingdom, they appeared with increased regularity. A thick, smoky haze hung over these places, smothering what little light could enter or leave. I would often gaze from the King's Highway in the quiet of the evening, and faintly hear the sounds of their misery — hateful voices, desperate cries, and sorrowful wailings.

It was such an evening, gazing at such a place when the guiding voice spoke to me in powerful clarity.

"Go." I hesitated, cautious to leave the King's Highway, but the voice was pure and the message persistent. "Go."

I guided my steed toward the dark village, and it went willingly. There was no warning voice, just a quiet peace confirming that this needed to be part of my journey.

The village I entered was small, just a handful of houses, but poverty and misery were everywhere. Four young children sat weeping beside a fresh mound of earth. There was no tombstone, no marker to record who was buried there. The children were covered in filth and little more than skeletons. As I walked my horse toward them, a brute of a man staggered out of the nearest house and bellowed a challenge. He cursed me and told me I was not wanted here. I looked again at the children.

"Are you the father of these children?"

"What business is it of yours?" he screamed at me. The children huddled together, terrified. I spoke to the oldest of them. "Is that your father?"

The boy looked at me, then back to the raving mad man.

"Son, look at me, not him. I promise he will not hurt you. Is that your father?"

In little more than a whisper he answered, "No." Then the dam burst, and in tears he wailed, "He killed our father, then moved into our home. He hurt our mother again and again, and now he's killed her!"

Something cold moved within me. I could feel the evil of this place, thick as fog. Two more men, brutes also, moved out of the shadows and joined the first. I could see that each held a weapon of sorts — one a sword, the other a spear, and the third a battered battle axe. I dismounted my horse and walked straight to them, stopping a few yards away.

"The child lies!" the man screamed.

"There is no reason for him to do so. He speaks the truth. I am here on the King's behalf, to execute his judgment and do his will. I am taking these children to a place where they will be loved and cared for. If one of you, or all of you, try to stop me, I will gladly avenge their parents' death."

I purposely turned my back to them and walked toward the children. After a few steps, the smallest girl screamed.

My sword came easily into my hand, and I have to say as I think back upon it, that I was glad they attacked. As I gazed at the fresh grave, I thought of my own mother. I imagined these children clawing out a place for theirs, saying their goodbyes, and burying her as best they could. I could have been born in this place just as easily as they. Pure evil had destroyed a man, tortured his wife, and ravaged these children. All that I felt went into my sword strokes, and never have I fought with such fury. Evil roared as they came, then screamed as they died. In less than a minute, three lives were taken and two were avenged.

I sheathed my blade and continued to the children. The oldest had covered the eyes of the three younger, so they were spared the sight of the carnage. I looked into his eyes.

"I am sorry you had to see that."

"I am not," he whispered. "I was glad to see it."

I could not imagine all they had suffered, and I had not a clue how to heal their hearts, but I knew who could. I knew where to take them.

I shared my food, and they ate like the starved. As they did, I told them of the King and his castle, and they looked as if they dared not believe me. I asked them if they would go with me, so that I could take them to this place. The three youngest looked at their brother. He stared hard into my eyes looking for deceit, then tears came, and he shook his head — yes.

It took three months for the five of us to travel back to the King's castle. They took turns riding my horse, or walking along side. The two youngest — boy-girl twins — never spoke but just stared at me wide-eyed when I talked to them. The second child — once her older brother scrubbed the mud from her face and hair — proved to be an adorable, curly-haired lass. She had an infectious laugh that made the journey pleasant. I passed the time by entertaining them with stories — the same ones my mother had told me as a child.

****

Hundreds of miles to the east, a lone figure rode a borrowed horse toward a castle he had left almost five years before. He was finally home. He stopped and stared for several minutes, then dismounted. Limping slightly, he led the horse the last mile.

The castle gate opened, and the lord of the castle burst onto the road on his fastest horse. He reined in, just in front of the weary traveler, slid from his horse, each facing the other. Private words were spoken, then the lord extended his hand. A firm handshake, then a father-son embrace. A long embrace.

And up on the ramparts, a mother watched, and wept, and whispered his name. "Angus."

Vala

As we crested the last hill, the four orphans grew quiet, all atop my horse, all staring in disbelief at the castle below. I smiled and brought them on. A trumpet sounded, and soon the King came to greet us. He went first to the children.

"Well, what have we here?" Not waiting for an answer, he called back to a servant at the gate, "Tell Vala I need her. Have her come quickly."

He then turned his attention to me. "Tell me, my son, what you have seen and what you have learned."

So much had happened. Where was I to start? "I know that I am not the same man who stood at this gate a year ago. I also know that, before I can become your warrior, I must first become your child — that orphans and outcasts are not the only ones who need a Father King."

"Good." His eyes intense. "What else?"

"That there is much good in the land — kind and wise people who helped me along my way and told me the things I needed to hear. But that there is also much evil, and it is destroying many lives in the kingdom."

"Did you find the dragon? Did you battle him?"

I bowed my head in shame. "In that I failed, my King. I searched but never found him — never took the battle to him."

"You are wrong." He smiled at my confusion. "You battled him every day. Every act of kindness — every widow helped, good deed done, smile given, soul encouraged — all was a victory against him. Every time you told someone of me, and helped them believe, you dealt the dragon a terrible blow. Failed? Hardly. You have proven yourself a worthy warrior."

I knelt before him, determined to serve him all my life.

"Now, tell me where you found these four."

So I did. Then added, "There is a vast part of the kingdom that is filled with villages like the one where I found them. Evil reigns and the people there are slaves to the sin it produces."

"Perhaps what they need is a good lord who will go there, build a castle, battle the evil, and spread the good news of the kingdom."

"Perhaps..." I answered, suddenly distracted. From the castle gate stepped a young woman who seemed strangely familiar, yet I was sure we had never met. Yes, she was fair to look upon, but there was something else about her. A glow, an aura, something... heavenly. Something so right.

She made her way to us, her eyes on the King. "You sent for me, my King?" There was a playful pleasantness about her.

"Yes, Vala. These children have traveled far. They will need to be cared for — from now on, this will be their home."

She smiled at the children, and they were enchanted by her. She then looked at me. The King spoke, because I suddenly could not. "This is my warrior prince. He rescued these children from the dragon."

She curtsied, then smiled at me. "You must be very brave." I opened my mouth as if to speak and still found no words, which seemed to amuse her. She turned, helped the children off the horse, scooped up the smallest girl, and then herded the others into the castle. I couldn't take my eyes off of her.

The King's eyes danced as he looked after her, then back to me. "If I could find a warrior prince to conquer this new territory, then I suppose it would be good for him to have a princess bride at his side." He shook his head and laughed. "Eventually, though, he would have to muster the courage to speak to her."

I scarcely heard his words as I stared after her. But I did hear two words clearly, spoken within, by my guiding voice.

"The One."

Other Books by the Author

Seven Royal Laws of Courtship
The Teenage Years of Jesus Christ
The Childhood Years of Jesus Christ
The 21 Tenets of Biblical Femininity
The 21 Tenets of Biblical Masculinity
Is Your Youth Group Dead or Alive?
Mountain Lessons
Grace Will Lead Me Home
104 Teen Bible Lessons
Did God Put a Book Inside of You?

Stay in the Castle Series

Stay in the Castle
The Warrior Prince
The Chosen One
The Prodigals

The Teenager's Guide Series

A Teenager's Guide to Character, Success & Happiness
A Teenager's Guide to the Invisible Creation
A Teenager's Guide to Healthy Relationships

Ultimate Goal Publications

Order by phone or online
(812) 665-4375
www.stayinthecastle.com